A Big, Spooky House

DONNA WASHINGTON

Illustrated by JACQUELINE ROGERS

Jump at the Sun
Hyperion Books for Children
New York

Once there was a man.

He was a **BIG** man.

He was a **STRONG** man!

And he knew it.

He went around picking fights with people just because
he knew he would win. He never walked away from trouble,
because he figured he could always battle his way out of it.

One day the people of his village told him that the army needed volunteers.

"Since you are a big, strong man," one of the ladies told him, "and you love to fight, you ought to see if you can fight in the army."

He thought about that for a minute, and then he said, "Yeah!"

He put his belongings on his back and started out down the road.

One of his neighbors hollered after him, "Hey, it's a long walk! Do you want me to give you a ride in my cart?"

He was a **BIG** man.

He was a **STRONG** man!

He said, "I'll walk."

As he was going across the countryside, he saw an inn. The innkeeper said, "Hey, it's going to rain this evening. Why don't you stop and stay in my inn for the night?"

He was a **BIG** man.

He was a **STRONG** man!

He said, "I don't care if I get wet."

He walked until the sun went down.

As soon as the sky was dark, there was an incredible peal of thunder. *BOOM!* The skies opened, and rain fell down in sheets.

He was a **BIG** man.

He was a **STRONG** man!

He was a wet man. He didn't like it one bit.

He was looking around trying to find someplace dry, when, in a flash of lightning, he saw a big, spooky house up on a hill.

Now, most people would have stayed away from that house. It was dark, and the gate was falling down. The windows were broken and the paint was peeling. There were holes in the roof and weeds growing all around the yard. Most people would have stayed away, but not him.

He was a **BIG** man.
He was a **STRONG** man!
He was a not-going-to-be-
scared-by-some-spooky-house-
sitting-up-on-a-big-spooky-hill
kind of man.

He went up to the door.

When he reached out for the doorknob, the door opened all by itself. *CREAK!*

Now, most people would have left there and then. But not him.

He was a **BIG** man.
He was a **STRONG** man!
He went right in.

Outside, the place was falling apart, but inside, it was beautiful.

There was a red carpet on the floor leading down a long hallway. Even though the windows were dark outside, there were candles burning in all of the candleholders. He looked around at the beautiful, dry, warm hallway and said, "Yeah!"

He followed the red carpet to the end of the hallway. There was a huge wooden door. He reached out to open it, but it opened by itself. *CREAK!*

Now, most people might have been more than just a little frightened by this, but not him.

He was a **BIG** man.

He was a **STRONG** man!

He went right into the room.

There was a huge fire with crackling logs. There was a huge stuffed chair facing the fire. In front of the chair was a table covered with lots of good things to eat. He just looked at everything and said, "Yeah!"

Now, some people would have been too terrified to eat, but not him.

He was a **BIG** man.
He was a **STRONG** man!
He sat down and got to work.

He had that table clear in no time. When he finished, he sat back and put his feet up on a little stool. When he opened his eyes, the table had disappeared. He looked around and said, "Yeah!"

He fell asleep in front of that fire. Fast asleep in that big comfortable chair until the clock on the wall began to chime. *BONG! BONG! BONG! BONG!*

It chimed twelve times. The man jumped up and said, "What! What! Oh, it's jest the clock."

The door behind him opened, and in came a black cat. Its fur was matted and dirty. Its eyes were as red as the fire. It came across the floor, scraping its claws across the wood. Its voice was thin and squeaky when it meowed. It walked over to the fireplace, jumped into the middle of the flames, picked up a flaming hot coal, and started to lick it. Then it looked straight at the man and said in a slow, screechy voice, "Are you gonna be here when John gets here?"

He was a **BIG** man.

He was a **STRONG** man!

He was a not-going-to-be-scared-by-any-cat-sitting-in-any-fireplace-licking-any-coal kind of man.

He stared into the fireplace and said, "I'll be here when John gets here and past that!" and he snapped his fingers to prove he didn't care.

He sat back in his chair and went back to sleep.

BONG!

The clock struck one. The man sat up. "What! WHAT! Oh, it's jest the clock."

The door behind him opened, and in came another black cat. This one was the size of a Doberman pinscher. It had black matted fur and fiery red eyes just like the other one. Its voice was deep and snarly.

It walked over to the fireplace, sat next to the other cat, picked up a log, bit off the end, and sat there crunching noisily. It looked out at the man and said in a slow, snarly voice, "Are you gonna be here when John gets here?"

He was a **BIG** man.

He was a **STRONG** man!

He was a worried man.

But he'd never run from anything in his life, and he wasn't about to start now. So he looked straight at that great big cat and said, "I'll be here when John gets here, and past that!" Then he snapped his fingers to prove he didn't care.

He looked around at the shadows of the room, and then added, "And I'm not scared!" He sat back in that chair, and truth be told, it took him quite a while to get back to sleep.

BONG! BONG!

The clock struck two. The man sat up. "What! What! Oh, it's jest the clock."

The door behind him opened, and in came another black cat. This one was the size of a large pony. Its hair was thick and matted with straw and sticks. Its eyes were bright red, and they were so big they gave off their own light. Its voice was deep, loud, and gravelly.

It walked over to the fireplace, ate up the other two cats, licked the fireplace clean, and then turned those glowing red eyes back toward that man. It opened its mouth to show two rows of long, needle-sharp teeth. Then it said to the man in a slow, deep, gravelly voice, "Are you gonna be here when John gets here?"

He was a **BIG** man!
He was a **STRONG** man!
He was a **GONE** man!

Author's Note

This is one of my favorite spooky stories. It has been making the rounds in the oral tradition for a very long time. I heard it for the first time almost twelve years ago as a short joke. Many people will recognize it by a number of other names—"Martin's Coming," or maybe "Pancho Villa," to name a couple. Usually, after I tell this story, a member of the audience will come up to me and announce they've heard something like it somewhere before. This is the version that I tell. I hope you will enjoy it and share it with someone else.

—D.W.

This book is for Devin,
who loves to be scared,
and David,
without whom life would be scary! —D.W.

For Elike and Adrian —J.R.

Visit www.jumpatthesun.com
Printed in Hong Kong by South China Printing Company, Ltd.
First Edition
1 3 5 7 9 10 8 6 4 2
The artwork for this book was prepared using watercolor.
This book is set in 16/23-point Caslon 224.
Library of Congress Cataloging-in-Publication Data on file.
Library of Congress Catalog Card Number 99-48443